To my very own Princess Amina:

You are strong. You are smart. You are important.
You are beautiful. You are brave. You are blessed.
And you are going to change the world.

Eres fuerte. Eres inteligente. Eres importante.
Eres bella. Eres valiente. Eres bendecida.
Y vas a cambiar el mundo.

MORE THAN A CROWN © copyright 2023 by ROBERTO CONCEPCIÓN, JR. All rights reserved. No part of this book may be reproduced in any form whatsoever, by photography or xerography or by any other means, by broadcast or transmission, by translation into any kind of language, nor by recording electronically or otherwise, without permission in writing from the author, except by a reviewer, who may quote brief passages in critical articles or reviews.

ISBN 13: 978-1-63489-949-9

Library of Congress Catalog Number has been applied for.
Printed in China
First Printing: 2023

27 26 25 24 23   5 4 3 2 1

Design by Jack Walgamuth

Wise Ink Creative Publishing
807 Broadway St. NE
Suite 46
Minneapolis, MN 55413

Never stop dreaming!
Roberto &
Amira

More Than a Crown

Written by **Roberto Concepción, Jr.**
Illustrated by **Anuki López**

Once upon a time, there lived four young princesses who were the bravest and kindest girls in all of the land:

Princess Nia
of the Naos Kingdom

Princess Sukhi
of the Sika Kingdom

Princess Eva
of the Elba Kingdom

and Princess Amina
of the Alya Kingdom.

They knew that when they grew up, they would rule their kingdoms. But each girl had a dream that extended past her crown.

One morning, Amina woke up excited.
It was the day of the royal tea party!
The other princesses could arrive at any moment.

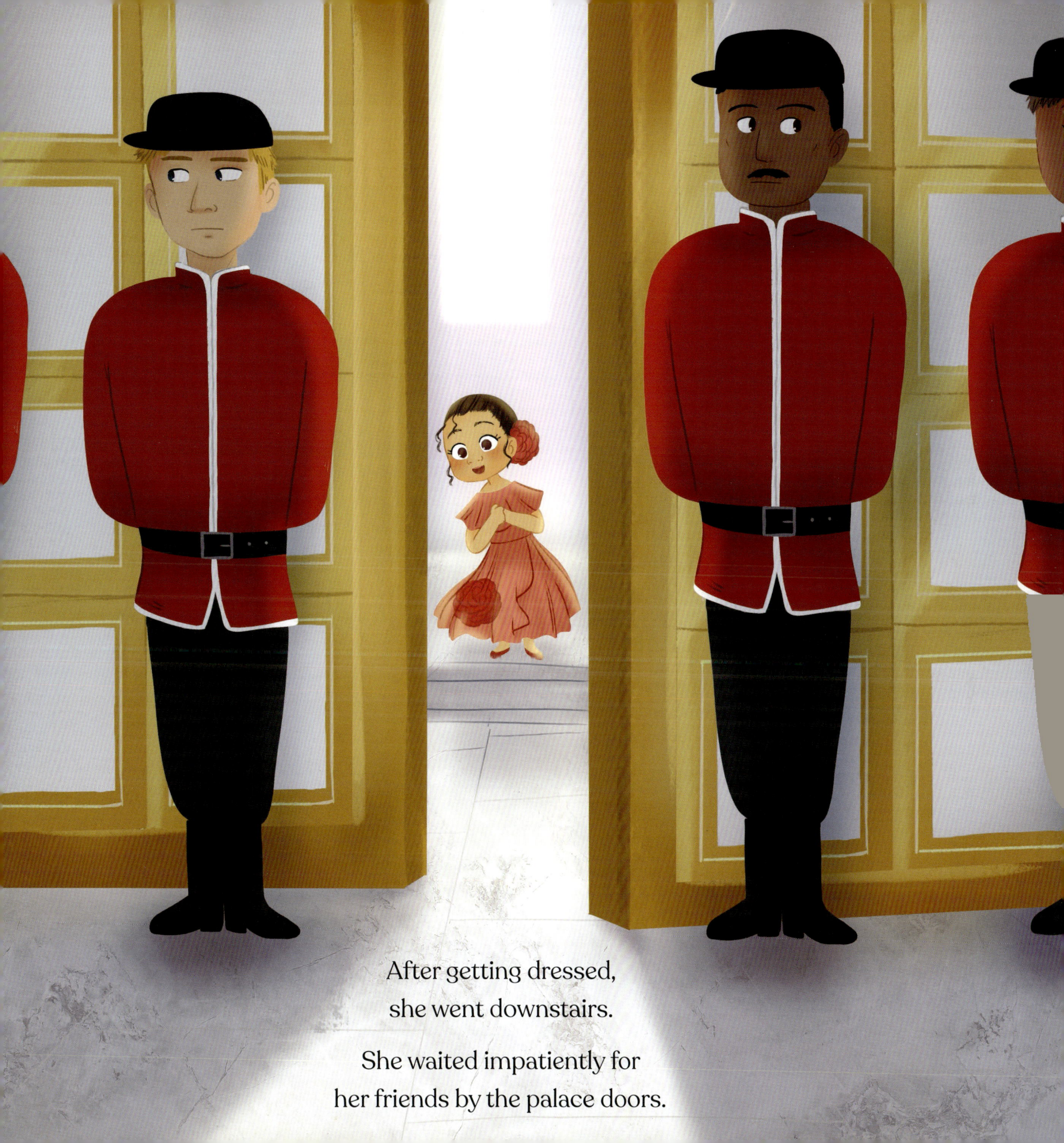

After getting dressed, she went downstairs.

She waited impatiently for her friends by the palace doors.

When the other princesses arrived, the four hugged each other tightly, but cautiously. Their parents had taught them the importance of presentation.

Nia checked the pins in her hair to make sure her bun remained intact.

Sukhi inspected her sari for any wrinkles.

And Eva, whose parents disapproved of public displays of affection, stepped back and curtsied.

Once out of sight of their parents, Amina leaned in close to the other princesses. She whispered, "Do you want to race to the end of the hall?"

Their eyes widened with excitement.

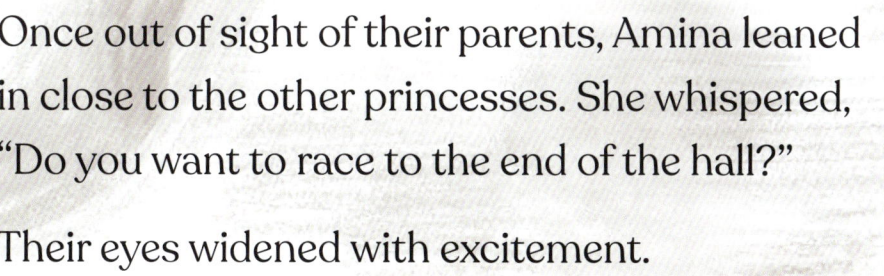

The girls took off, sliding along the polished floor.

They were having fun until they bumped into a royal official. He disapprovingly said, "Now, now. Let's not forget to act like princesses."

The princesses looked down at the floor, embarrassed, before walking into the drawing room.

Amina frowned and then said, "We ARE princesses! We were just having fun."

Soon the tea arrived, and with it, the princesses' families.
"Don't take the first scone, honey," said Amina's grandmother.
"A princess always lets her guests go first."

"Watch your sari, and sit up straight, Sukhi,"
said Sukhi's mom. "A princess doesn't slouch."

"Pass the finger sandwiches to your right, not your left," said Eva's mom.

"Nia, where is your napkin?" asked Nia's dad. "You should always put your napkin on your lap before you start eating."

With their spirits low, the princesses excused themselves. They went to Amina's room. Once she closed her bedroom door, Amina said, "That tea party was the worst!"

Nia responded, "I know, but being a princess isn't always fun. So much is expected of us." She pointed at her freshly styled hair. "Like this," she said. "I'm more than the hair on my head."

Sukhi followed, looking down at the sari she was wearing. "I'm more than what I wear."

Knowing that she would be expected to marry a prince when she was older, Eva chimed in. "I'm more than the person I marry. But . . . it feels like we don't have much say."

"That's not true," Amina said. "We're all more than what's expected of us! I am a princess, but I also want to be an astronaut when I grow up. I want to explore Mars."

Eva was shocked. "But won't your kingdom miss you?"

"I will make them proud by advancing science," said Amina.

The other princesses were inspired and thought about the marks they would like to leave on the world.

"When I grow up, I want to be a scientist.
I'll find cures to make people feel better," said Eva.

"When I grow up, I want to be an architect. I'll design the tallest sustainable building in the world," said Sukhi.

"And when I grow up, I want to be a pilot. I'll travel to new places and learn about different cultures," Nia said.

The princesses smiled as they thought about the differences they would make in the world.

Ever the dreamer, Sukhi asked, "What if we lived in kingdoms that saw us for more than our crowns?"

Eva, who loved to solve problems, suggested, "What if we meet with our parents and find a solution together?"

The history buff of the group, Nia, thought about lessons learned from former kingdoms and pondered, "What if we try what worked for others in the past?"

Amina, the adventure seeker of the group, considered this unknown territory for them to explore. "What if we did all three?" she suggested with a smile.

"I have an idea!"

After the princesses agreed on their plan, they hurried to the great hall, where the royal families were meeting to discuss global affairs. While on their way, they ran into the royal official yet again.

"Why are you in such a rush?" he asked.

"We're declaring our independence!" they said together.

The official laughed and said, "You cannot be serious. Your job is to look impeccable and make sure the kingdom falls in love with you. That's it!"

Amina stomped her foot and responded,

"We'll show you!"

The princesses continued to the great hall and knocked on the door. When the door opened, Amina's dad, the king of the Alya Kingdom, invited them inside. Their moment had arrived! With her head held high and her friends by her side, Amina read from her scroll.

"We hereby request consideration of the following Declaration of Independence for immediate recognition."

Eva continued, "We hold these truths to be self-evident."

"That all children are created equal," read Nia.

"That they are endowed with certain rights, that among these are the right to self-expression," followed Sukhi.

"The right to love whomever they choose," said Eva.

"And the right to follow their dreams," ended Amina.

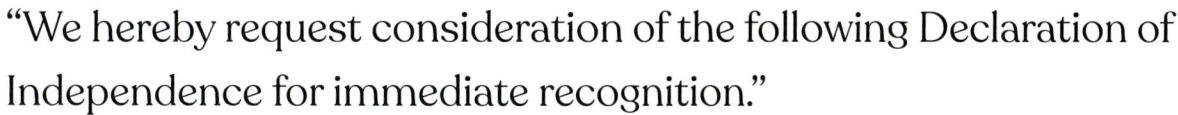

The king looked to the royal families to his left and right.

"Self-expression?" said a royal official.

"Your responsibility is to express the will of the people!"

But the king held up his hand. "That responsibility was never intended to be limiting. To reign is to serve, oneself included," he said.

There were some murmurs among the royal officials.
Then, one by one, the families nodded their consent.

The king, beaming with pride, said aloud,

"So ordered!"

The princesses jumped for joy!

They thanked the royal court and were ready to excuse themselves when the king asked to speak with Amina.

Once out of earshot, the king looked into her eyes and said, "My love, **being a princess is a privilege, but being more than a princess is your destiny.** Follow your dreams wherever they may take you. You made me a very proud papa today." The king kissed the top of her head and then left to return to the royal meeting.

Amina smiled from ear to ear.

She then reunited with her friends so they could enjoy their own tea party in peace.

After the princesses entered Amina's room, they sat at a table set with their favorite teacups and snacks. Amina lifted her teacup and toasted, "To us!" as the princesses clinked their cups.

The possibilities were endless for them.
Their imaginations were their only limit.
From that moment on, they lived happily
ever after—with their crowns *and* their dreams.

A note for caregivers

When we dream, we envision a world beyond our reality, where the possibilities are endless and extraordinary. As caregivers, encouraging our children to follow their dreams is one of the greatest gifts we can offer them. Research shows that encouragement has beneficial effects on a child's motivation. Encouragement from adults cultivates a growth mindset, leading to an increased desire to learn, more task persistence and better performance (even after failure), higher self-esteem, and the belief in improvement through effort.

While this book is intended for all children, for parents of girls (like myself), the importance of encouragement cannot be stressed enough. At a young age, girls are shaped by gender stereotypes in the world around them—for example, negative stereotypes that could discourage them from participating in science, technology, engineering, and math (STEM). Studies have shown that gender stereotypes influence children's motivation, including their beliefs around their own abilities and sense of belonging. This correlation is even stronger for girls of color, who are the least likely to report a sense of belonging in industries where women are underrepresented, such as in STEM fields. When children are free to challenge stereotypes and see others do the same, they are more likely to believe in their own potential and try things that interest them without giving undue weight to their mistakes and others' opinions. As caregivers, we have the responsibility to help our children develop a positive self-image. Given the proven role of children's literature in shaping self-image, this includes exposing our children, particularly those of color, to literature in which they can see themselves represented.

I hope that reading or listening to this story will inspire your child to reflect on how they can make their unique mark on the world—just like Princess Amina and her friends—and move you to encourage your child to be their ancestors' wildest dreams.

Busch, Bradley. "Research every teacher should know: growth mindset." The Guardian. January 4, 2018. https://www.theguardian.com/teacher-network/2018/jan/04/research-every-teacher-should-know-growth-mindset.

Cvencek, David, Andrew N. Meltzoff, and Anthony G. Greenwald. "Math—Gender Stereotypes in Elementary School Children." Child Development 82, no. 3 (May/June 2011): 766-779. https://doi.org/10.1111/j.1467-8624.2010.01529.x.

Hurley, Dorothy L. "Seeing White: Children of Color and the Disney Fairy Tale Princess." The Journal of Negro Education 74, no. 3 (Summer 2005): 221-232. https://www.jstor.org/stable/40027429.

Law, Fidelia, Luke McGuire, Mark Winterbottom, and Adam Rutland. "Children's Gender Stereotypes in STEM Following a One-Shot Growth Mindset Intervention in a Science Museum." Frontiers in Psychology (May 10, 2021). https://doi.org/10.3389/fpsyg.2021.641695.

Master, Allison. "Gender Stereotypes Influence Children's STEM Motivation." Child Development Perspectives 15, no. 3 (September 2021): 203-210. https://doi.org/10.1111/cdep.12424.

Mueller, CM and Dweck, CS. "Praise for intelligence can undermine children's motivation and performance." Journal of Personality and Social Psychology 75, no. 1 (July 1998): 33-52. DOI: 10.1037//0022-3514.75.1.33.

Raincy, Katherine, Melissa Dancy, Roslyn Mickelson, Elizabeth Stearns, and Stephanie Moller. "Race and gender differences in how sense of belonging influences decisions to major in STEM." International Journal of STEM Education 5, no. 1 (April 2018) 10. DOI: 10.1186/s40594-018-0115-6.

About the Author

Roberto Concepción, Jr., always knew he wanted to be a father. Inspired by the birth of his daughter, Roberto wrote *More Than a Crown* to encourage her—and other children around the world—to follow their dreams and reach for the stars. This is his first book.

For more information, visit MoreThanaCrownBook.com.

About the Illustrator

Anuki López is a Spanish illustrator who has been drawing since she can remember—a notebook and colored pencils were her favorite toys. Once she grew up, she studied art and graphic design at university. In her final year, she discovered the fantastic world of children's illustration and fell in love with it. She loves working and living her life as an illustrator, bringing children illustrations that are full of color, magic, humor, animals, respect, and, of course, love.